T.R. Bear

T.R.'s DAY OUT

T.R. Bear

T.R.'s DAY OUT

Terrance Dicks

Illustrated by
Susan Hellard

Barron's
New York

First edition for the United States and the Philippines published
1988 by Barron's Educational Series, Inc.

First published 1985 by Piccadilly Press Ltd., London, England

All inquiries should be addressed to:
Barron's Educational Series, Inc.
250 Wireless Boulevard
Hauppauge, New York 11788

Library of Congress Catalog Card No. 88-16768

International Standard Book No. 0-8120-4107-0

Library of Congress Cataloging-in-Publication Data

Dicks, Terrance.
    T.R.'s day out.

    (T.R. Bear)
    Summary: Jimmy takes his Teddy Roosevelt bear
and his other talking toys to the American exhibit
at the British Museum where they foil the robbery
of a portrait of the real Teddy Roosevelt.
    [1. Mystery and detective stories. 2. Teddy
bears—Fiction. 3. Toys—Fiction] I. Hillard,
Susan, ill. II. Title. III. Title: TR's day out.
IV. Series: Dicks, Terrance. T.R. Bear.
PZ7.D5627Day   1988   [E]   88-16768
ISBN 0-8120-4107-0

PRINTED IN THE UNITED STATES OF AMERICA
901 977 987654321

CONTENTS

Chapter One

An Outing for T.R.

"You've got to take me. You've just got to," pleaded T.R. "What are you trying to do, stop my cultural development? I've just gotta see that exhibition!"

"It was a pretty unusual request to come from a teddy bear," thought Jimmy. But then, T.R. was a pretty unusual bear.

To begin with, he could talk. Not just pretend talk, the way lots of children do with their toys, but really talk.

T.R. could come to life.

As a matter of fact, all toys can come to life, but they're not supposed to do it until their owners are safely asleep.

T.R. was inclined to break the rules when he felt like it.

Perhaps it was because he was an American bear, sent over in a package by Jimmy's Uncle Colin in the United States.

You could tell T.R. was different just by looking at him. For a start he wore a checked jacket, a bow tie, and round wire glasses with no glass. Instead of being round and cuddly, T.R. looked tough and determined.

T.R. was a bear who liked to get things done.

What he wanted to get done at the moment was to persuade Jimmy to take him with him on tomorrow's school trip to the British Museum. There was an American Exhibition on, and T.R. was desperate to see it.

They were having their whispered conversation, or rather argument, in Jimmy's bedroom, just after bedtime.

The minute Jimmy's mom had come and kissed him goodnight and turned off the light, T.R. had jumped down from the toy shelf onto Jimmy's bed, marched up to the pillow, and started talking.

He had heard about the coming trip during the day—even when he

wasn't talking, T.R. was always listening—and now he was determined to go along.

"Come on, Jimmy," he pleaded. "What do you say?"

"I say, old chap, do stop making a pest of yourself," drawled a superior-sounding voice.

It was Edward, Jimmy's other teddy

bear, as British as T.R. was American. Once T.R. started talking the other toys usually joined in as well, as if they'd decided it was no use trying to keep their secret any longer.

"After all," Edward went on, "who wants to go to some boring old museum anyway?"

"That's not the right attitude," said a stern female voice. "A good museum is an educational experience. Even T.R. knows that. And if he's going, then I'm certainly going as well!"

Jimmy groaned into his pillow. You might think it was great fun having toys that came alive and talked to you, and of course, in a lot of ways, it was. The trouble was, his toys didn't just talk, they argued, not just with each other, but with him.

"Christopher Robin never had all this trouble with Winnie-the-Pooh," thought Jimmy. "All his toys ever did was stand around telling him how wonderful he was!"

The female voice came from the third toy in the room, a rag doll called Sally Ann that Jimmy had inherited from his sister Jenny. Sally Ann was a strong supporter of something she called "Doll's Lib," which meant she was quite determined not to be put down or left out just because she was "only a doll."

"Sure thing, Sally Ann," said T.R. generously. "Glad to have you along. You can be my guide, give me the tour."

They were both taking it for granted they were going by now, thought Jimmy. No one was asking *him*.

Jimmy sat up. "Now wait a minute, you two. How am I supposed to explain taking a teddy bear and a rag doll on a trip to the British Museum?

I can hardly say they want to improve their cultural development."

"No problem," said T.R. briskly. "Me and Sally Ann'll ride in that big old book bag of yours."

"You won't see much from in there, will you?"

"Sure we will. We can just pop our heads out when no one's around."

"There won't *be* a time when no one's around," Jimmy pointed out. "And if you think I'm going to lug two talking toys around all day . . ."

"Three," said Edward Bear's reproachful voice.

T.R. swung around. "I thought you didn't want to come to some boring old museum?"

"Well, perhaps I was a shade hasty. I mean, you wouldn't leave a chap here all alone, would you?"

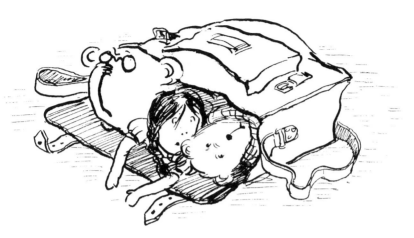

And so it was settled—somehow—without any reference to Jimmy. They were *all* going.

And that was that!

* * *

"That looks like a pretty full book bag to me," said Jimmy's brother George as Jimmy left the house next morning. "What on earth have you got in there?"

"Oh, supplies—notebooks, stuff like that," said Jimmy airily.

George gave him his older brother type superior look. "You're only going to the British Museum, you know. You're not exploring darkest Africa. Let's have a look."

George made a grab for the book bag, but Jimmy snatched it away. "You mind your own business," he said, and slipped past George and out of the front door.

As he hurried along to school, Jimmy could hear a sort of muffled chorus coming from inside the book bag.

"I say, old chap, you might give a fellow a bit of room."

That was Edward Bear.

Then a female voice. "Come on, move over a bit, T.R., there's a good chap."

This was Sally Ann.

Then there came T.R.'s low
rumble. "Listen, Sally Ann, I've got
your elbow in my ribs and Edward's
foot in my ear. I'm the one who
ought to be complaining."

"You're the one who's taking up all the room," grumbled Edward.

"That's right," said Sally Ann. "Some people are rather bulkier than others, you know!"

"Listen, nobody invited you two guys along. There's plenty of room back up on the toy shelf."

By now the noise from the book bag was quite loud.

Suddenly, Nick, one of Jimmy's school friends, ran up to join him. "What's all that noise coming from inside your book bag? Have you got a radio playing in there or something?"

Jimmy went red. "Must have switched itself on by accident. You go on, Nick and I'll fix it."

Nick ran ahead, and Jimmy leaned down, opened his school bag, and hissed, "Now listen, all of you, be quiet—or I'll stick this bag in the school coatroom and leave it there all day."

He ran on and caught up with Nick.

When they reached the school, the mini-bus was standing in the playground with most of the class already inside.

Mr. Briskin, Jimmy's teacher, was running around and around like a dog chasing its tail. He was a thin, fair-haired young man, quite nice most of the time, but he was really too nervous and excitable to be a teacher. When things got too much for him, he sometimes got into a real tizzy.

He was in a tizzy now, because it

was almost time for the mini-bus to leave and not everyone was inside yet. History had been Mr. Briskin's major at the university, and he'd been preparing them for months for this visit.

When Jimmy and Nick appeared, he started jumping up and down with anxiety. "There you are," he squawked. "Get in, get in, get in!" He stood in the doorway and looked around the bus. "Now then, that's everyone, isn't it?"

Jimmy looked around too. "Everyone except Timmy, sir."

Timmy was the smallest boy in the class, so small that everyone called him Mouse.

Mr. Briskin exploded. "I might have known it would be him. He's always late. Well, we will have to go without him. We've got a very full timetable today, and I can't be expected to—"

Jimmy tugged at Mr. Briskin's sleeve. "Sir! *Sir!*"

Mr. Briskin glared down at him. "What is it, boy?"

Jimmy pointed. Mouse was standing at the door of the mini-bus, peering up at them through his glasses, too terrified to get on.

Mr. Briskin gulped. "All right, Timmy," he said, quite kindly. "Don't just stand there, get on!"

Mouse scurried to a seat at the back of the mini-bus, and Jimmy and Nick sat down together.

Mr. Briskin looked around and took a final head count—actually, he took two, because he counted wrong the first time. Finally he got it right and sat down in the front, nodding to the driver. They were on their way!

Chapter Two

The Fake

It was a short but lively journey to the British Museum.

There was quite a bit of shouting and fooling around from the class because they were excited, and quite a lot of yelling from Mr. Briskin

because he was even more nervous than usual.

Mr. Briskin hated school trips, even more than he hated playground duty. His idea of a teacher's life was standing in a classroom teaching a quiet, well-behaved class, something which very seldom seemed to come his way.

The mini-bus driver seemed quite relieved by the time he pulled up on the pavement outside the British Museum and let them all out. He drove away after faithfully promising to return at three o'clock to pick them up. The plan was that they

would spend all day at the museum—everyone had been told to bring lunch and some money for snacks.

Mr. Briskin lined them all up. "Right, everybody follow me. First stop, the Egyptians!" He paused, looking around the class. "Now remember, the British Museum's a big place, a *very* big place, very easy to get lost in, and knowing all of you, someone's almost certain to manage it. Try and stay with the class, but if you do get lost, just remember to be here, outside the main entrance at three o'clock. Otherwise, you'll have to find your own way home!"

19

Then, like Napoleon at the head of his troops, Mr. Briskin led the class up the steps and into the museum.

* * *

"Well, it's certainly big all right," thought Jimmy as he stood with the others, staring around the huge entrance hall.

Perhaps because it was a weekday morning the museum wasn't very busy yet, and Mr. Briskin and his class seemed lost in the big echoing space.

But Mr. Briskin was experienced when it came to the museum. Confidently he led them up the stairs, along echoing corridors, and into the main Egyptian Gallery.

"We'll start off with the funeral ornaments," he announced. "When one of the Egyptian kings died it was customary to bury his treasure with him so he could make an impressive arrival into the other world . . ."

He led them past towering mummy cases toward a glass case filled with jewels and ornaments.

Jimmy was trailing along behind, since he didn't find dead Egyptians all that fascinating.

Suddenly, he heard a voice from inside his book bag. "Get lost, kid!"

Jimmy looked down. "No need to be rude, T.R." he whispered.

"I mean, deliberately," growled T.R. "We're never going to get to see anything trailing around after this mob!"

Jimmy glanced at the others, all crowded dutifully around Mr. Briskin, then edged backwards out of the door.

Once in the corridor he undid his book bag. He looked around. For the moment the corridor was empty, "All right, it's all clear," he whispered.

Immediately T.R.'s head popped out of the bag, then Edward Bear's, then Sally Ann's.

"All right," said Jimmy. "Where now?"

Immediately, an argument broke out.

Edward wanted to see suits of armor and ancient weapons. "Part of my British heritage, you know," he said grandly.

Sally Ann called Edward a male chauvinist bear. "I would like to see something rather more artistic. Greek statues, ancient vases, that sort of thing."

T.R. let out a howl of protest.

"Listen, you guys, let's not forget why we came here," he growled. "The special American Art Exhibition, remember?"

"T.R.'s right," said Jimmy firmly. "He was the one who wanted to come to the museum in the first place. You two will have to wait your turn."

A museum guard turned into the corridor, and immediately the three little heads disappeared inside the bag again.

Half opening the bag, Jimmy went up to him and asked him the way to the American Exhibition, and the man began reeling off a long and complicated string of directions.

The American Exhibition turned out to be in a little side gallery at the end of a corridor on the far side of the museum.

A sign on a stand outside the gallery explained that it was a traveling exhibition, sponsored by the American government, and that it was due to spend a few weeks in all the different capitals of Europe.

At the moment the little gallery was completely empty.

Jimmy unfastened his book bag and set it down on the floor. "All right, now's your chance. You can get out and have a look around, while I keep watch in the doorway. If anyone comes I'll have time to give you a shout, and you can jump back inside the bag again."

T.R. was out of the bag and marching across the floor almost before Jimmy had finished speaking, and, a little more cautiously, Edward Bear and Sally Ann climbed out and followed him.

Jimmy stood by the door, keeping watch.

As it turned out, there was something for everyone in the American Exhibition.

Sally Ann found a display case full of the most beautiful American Indian embroidery—moccasins and pouches and clothes decorated with brightly colored beads. She particularly liked the sign in the case, pointing out the importance of the squaws in preserving the tribe's artistic heritage.

Edward stood studying an exhibition rack of "Guns that Won the West." He pulled an imaginary cowboy hat down over his eyes, and Jimmy guessed he was imagining himself as Buffalo Bill or Billy the Kid. As for T.R., there was only one exhibit in the gallery as far as he was concerned.

It was a painting, a full-length portrait hanging on the wall. It showed a rather tubby-looking little man sitting on a big white horse. He wore a vaguely cowboyish sort of outfit, there was a cartridge belt strapped round his waist, and he was carrying a rifle.

The man was staring ahead with a grim, determined look on his face, and he wore a pair of round glasses.

T.R. marched straight up to the painting and stood staring up at it, an almost worshipful expression on his face. Somehow, the man in the painting seemed to be staring straight back at him.

Jimmy went over and stood beside T.R., and for a moment they stood looking at the picture together.

Jimmy looked down at the fascinated T.R. "Is that who I think it is?"

T.R. nodded, pointing to the sign beside the picture.

It read: "Theodore Roosevelt, at the time he raised his famous troop of Rough Riders to fight in the Cuban War in 1898."

"Yep," said T.R. reverently. "That was three years before he became president, of course."

Jimmy knew that Theodore Roosevelt, Teddy for short, was T.R.'s great hero. Not surprisingly, since, according to T.R., all teddy bears were actually named after Teddy Roosevelt. Anyway, T.R. did his best to model himself after his hero, and even wore the same kind of round glasses to be more like him.

Suddenly a voice boomed out behind them. "Howdy there, little pardner!"

Jimmy swung round, horrified. He had forgotten to keep watch in the doorway, and now someone had come in—with the toys alive and moving about.

And what a someone!

The newcomer was small, but amazingly fat. He wore a flowered Hawaiian shirt ballooned out by his enormous belly, and there was a complicated-looking camera hanging

around his neck. He wore cowboy
boots and an enormous cowboy
hat.

Jimmy glanced down quickly and
saw that T.R. was lying flat on his
back, staring glassy-eyed at the ceiling,
looking just like an ordinary toy.

Quickly, Jimmy bent down and

snatched the little bear up. A quick glance around showed him that Sally Ann and Edward Bear were nowhere to be seen.

"Admiring good old Teddy Roosevelt, I see," said the fat man. "Gee, but he sure was some swell guy. Greatest president we ever had in the little old U.S. of A."

"I'm sure he was," said Jimmy politely, and began backing away.

If he could pick up the other toys without the man noticing . . .

Tucking T.R. under his arm, Jimmy started edging toward the other end of the room.

Suddenly, a voice from around his arm muttered, "Hold it, kid, there's something funny going on here. This guy's a fake!"

Chapter Three

Robbery!

The fat man swung around and glared suspiciously at Jimmy. "What was that, pardner?"

"I didn't say anything!"

"Oh, yes, you did. Something about a fake."

The man looked suddenly threatening, almost dangerous.

"Oh, I was just sort of thinking out loud," said Jimmy hurriedly. "Wondering if that painting could be a fake."

The man shook his head. "Oh, it's no fake, believe me. Matter of fact, it's a newly discovered portrait, been hidden away for years. It's worth a heck of a lot of money."

"That's very interesting," said Jimmy. "Well, I must be going . . ."

T.R. was right, decided Jimmy. There was something very odd about this man. Perhaps he'd better wait outside and get the other toys later, when the man had gone.

Clutching the now silent T.R., Jimmy slipped out of the door.

As soon as they were out in the corridor, T.R. came to life again.

"We've got to stick around, kid,"

he growled. "That guy's as phony as a three-dollar bill. If you ask me, he's planning a heist."

Jimmy stared at him. "A what?"

"A robbery! That's it! He's planning to hijack Teddy Roosevelt's portrait!"

"He did say it was worth a lot of money," said Jimmy thoughtfully. "But what makes you so sure? He could be just an innocent tourist."

T.R. shook his head. "Not a chance. I tell you the guy's a fake."

"How can you tell?"

"The way he talks, the way he's dressed."

"Like an American tourist?"

Once again, T.R. shook his head. "Like an Englishman's idea of an American tourist. The shirt, the hat, the boots, the camera, the accent—all together and all overdone."

"Well, you ought to know, T.R. But if he is planning a crime, he's made himself pretty noticeable. Anyway, what do we do now?"

"We sneak back in there. There's a display case just to the left of the door. If we duck behind that we can keep an eye on him."

Jimmy hesitated, and T.R. said, "Look, we've got to go back in there sometime. Sally Ann and Edward are still inside. Oh, and put me down, will you?" As usual, once T.R. took charge, there didn't seem anything to do but obey.

T.R. slipped through the door, and seconds later Jimmy followed.

They both crouched behind the display case and peered cautiously out.

The fat man was standing in front of the Roosevelt portrait, studying it almost greedily.

He glanced quickly around the room, and Jimmy and T.R. ducked back, afraid he'd see them, but they must have moved just in time.

When they peeped out again, the fat man had gone back to studying the painting. Then he started to move.

He took off his cowboy hat, and then his cowboy boots, revealing ordinary white tennis shoes underneath.

He took off his flashy Hawaiian shirt.

And then, to their amazement, he took off his stomach!

Suddenly the fat tourist had vanished, and in his place was a thin man in a black T-shirt, jeans and tennis shoes, someone you wouldn't look at twice.

"Everyone would have noticed him coming in," thought Jimmy, "but no one would realize it was the same man going out."

The little man leaned over his removed "stomach." As they could now see, it was a sort of stomach-shaped bag, more or less like a backpack, held on by straps and worn on the front instead of the back.

They watched fascinated as he took a number of objects out of the disguised container.

The first was a neatly printed sign. It read:

AMERICAN EXHIBITION
TEMPORARILY CLOSED

They ducked out of sight once again as the man hurried past their hiding place and popped outside, presumably to put the sign on the stand outside the door. He then hurried back to the bag.

Next he took out a small metal black box with controls set in the lid. He glanced around the room until he located an electrical fuse box in the far corner of the room. He hurried over to it and attached the black box. A light began flashing in its lid.

"A circuit breaker to fix the alarms," whispered T.R. "This guy's a real pro."

Next the robber went up to the painting and lifted it carefully down from its hook, resting it against the wall. No alarm bells rang, so his black box gimmick must have been working.

The next thing to come out of the bag was a knife with a long, thin blade.

"He's going to cut the painting out of the frame," growled T.R. "Give me some kind of distraction, kid!"

Jimmy thought for a moment, fished a penny out of his pocket, and pitched it over to the other side of the room.

It fell with a tiny clatter, and the robber whirled around, staring at the place the sound had come from.

Seeing no one was there, he turned his attention back to the painting . . .

Suddenly Jimmy realized that T.R. was no longer beside him.

Looking around, he saw some movement on the other side of the room. But it wasn't T.R.

It was Edward Bear and Sally Ann, creeping slowly toward the corner fuse box.

The robber picked up his knife and moved forward, preparing to cut the painting from its frame.

Just as the knife was about to touch the canvas a voice boomed, "STOP!"

The robber leaped backward in shock.

The voice seemed to be coming from the portrait itself.

On the other side of the room,

Edward Bear and Sally Ann had just
reached the fuse box.

Unfortunately, it was just too high
on the wall for them to reach.

As Jimmy watched, Sally Ann began
climbing on Edward's shoulders.

Nervously, the thief approached the painting again.

As he reached out with his knife, the voice boomed out again, "You heard me! Keep your thieving hands away from my portrait!"

From the back of his white horse, Teddy Roosevelt seemed to glare accusingly at the man, who stared at the talking painting in utter amazement.

Jimmy grinned. There was only the tiniest space between the painting and the wall against which it was now leaning.

No room for a man to hide, or even a child. But plenty of room for a very small bear with a very big voice.

Springing forward, the robber lifted the painting to one side.

There behind it stood T.R. Bear,

hands on hips and jaw stuck out,
looking every bit as tough and
determined as his famous namesake
on the white horse.

"Beat it, you lowdown, mangy
rascal," he roared. "Before I call the
cops."

For a moment the robber stared at
T.R. in amazement. Then, as if in
panic, he leaped forward, slashing
with the knife.

T.R. ducked, and the robber raised
his knife to strike again.

Balancing on Edward Bear's
shoulders, Sally leaped up and
grabbed the circuit breaker,
wrenching it free from the fuse box.
Sally Ann and Edward Bear fell to the
ground, but the circuit breaker came
with them.

Suddenly the little gallery was filled with the clanging of the alarm bell.

Now thoroughly panic-stricken, the thief ran for the door.

Jimmy decided it was time that *he* did something.

Dashing forward, he threw himself on his hands and knees in front of the fleeing robber, who fell forward over Jimmy's bent back and crashed to the ground.

Half-dazed he climbed to his feet and staggered forward—straight into the arms of two strong museum guards who came rushing through the door.

The thief struggled furiously, and Jimmy used the distraction to grab T.R., Sally Ann, and Edward and shove them back in his book bag.

"Well done, kid," whispered T.R. "Teddy Roosevelt would have been proud of you. Now, let's get out of here!"

Chapter Four

T.R.'s Reward

As Jimmy headed for the door, one of the struggling museum guards called out, "Hang on a minute, sonny. What's going on here?"

Jimmy paused in the doorway. "Don't ask me. All I know is, I came in here to take a look at the exhibition, and that guy dashed out and fell over me. Sorry, I must go now. I've lost the school group I'm with and I'll be in for it if I don't find them again! You can have all the credit."

Before the museum guard could say any more, Jimmy turned and ran. As he hurried along the corridor, Jimmy couldn't help laughing at the thought of the would-be robber's astonished face.

Still, he'd probably keep very quiet about what had really happened. Bad enough being captured by a kid. How much worse to have to admit to being captured by a kid, two teddy bears, and a rag doll.

* * *

Jimmy arrived at the Egyptian room just as Mr. Briskin and the rest of the class were leaving. "Where on earth have you been, Jimmy?" demanded Mr. Briskin. Luckily, he didn't wait for an answer. "Come along now, we're just about to set off for the Greek gallery, then I thought we might look at some medieval arms and armor."

"Be right with you, sir," said Jimmy cheerfully.

He was undoing his book-bag and sitting the three toys up inside so they'd have a good view of whatever was going on in the museum. Mr. Briskin stared at him in astonishment. "May I ask why you've brought those three toys with you, Jimmy?"

After such an eventful morning, Jimmy was past caring about whether anyone might think him crazy.

"I thought it might be educational

for them, sir. This lady is called Sally
Ann, and this bear is Edward. I
believe you've already met
T.R.?"

"Yes, of course, how do you do?"
said Mr. Briskin, leaning forward to
shake hands. He checked himself,
suddenly realizing he was having a
conversation with a teddy bear—or
trying to, anyway.

Edward Bear and Sally Ann and, of course, T.R. brought up the rear, peering out of Jimmy's book bag.

And they didn't miss a thing.

After all, everyone knows that teddy bears can't talk.

Can they?

"All the same," thought Mr. Briskin, "there was something rather mysterious about that bear . . ."

T.R. stared blandly at Mr. Briskin.

Just for a moment, Mr. Briskin could have sworn that T.R. *winked.* Absolutely impossible, of course. It must have been just a trick of the light.

Mr. Briskin took a deep breath.

"This way, class," he called, and led the expedition on its way.

More Fun, Mystery, And Adventure With Goliath–

Goliath And The Burglar

The first Goliath story tells how David persuades his parents to buy him a puppy. When Goliath grows very big it appears that he might have to leave the household. David is worried—until a burglar enters the house, and Goliath becomes a hero! (Paperback, ISBN 3820-7—Library Binding, ISBN 5823-2)

Goliath And The Buried Treasure

When Goliath discovers how much fun it is to dig holes, both he and David get into trouble with the neighbors. Meanwhile, building developers have plans that will destroy the city park—until Goliath's skill at digging transforms him into the most unlikely hero in town! (Paperback, ISBN 3819-3—Library Binding, ISBN 5822-4)

Goliath On Vacation

David persuades his parents to bring Goliath with them on vacation—but the big hound quickly disrupts life at the hotel. Goliath is in trouble with David's parents, but he soon redeems himself when he helps David solve the mystery of the disappearing ponies. (Paperback, ISBN 3821-5—Library Binding, ISBN 5824-0)

Goliath At The Dog Show

Goliath helps David solve the mystery at the dog show—then gets a special prize for his effort! (Paperback, ISBN 3818-5—Library Binding, ISBN 5821-6)

Goliath's Christmas

Goliath plays a big part in rescuing a snow storm victim. Then he and David join friends for the best Christmas party ever. (Paperback, ISBN 3878-9—Library Binding, ISBN 5843-7)

Goliath's Easter Parade

With important help from Goliath, David finds a way to save the neighborhood playground by raising funds at the Easter Parade. (Paperback, ISBN 3957-2—Library Binding, ISBN 5877-1)

Written by Terrance Dicks and illustrated by Valerie Littlewood, all Goliath books at bookstores. Or order direct from Barron's. Paperbacks $2.95 each, Library Bindings $7.95 each. When ordering direct from Barron's, please indicate ISBN number and add 10% postage and handling (Minimum $1.50). N.Y. residents add sales tax.

250 Wireless Boulevard, Hauppauge, N.Y. 11788
Call toll-free: 1-800-645-3476, in NY 1-800-257-5729

BARRON'S